The Super Soccer Game

Written by Christine Ricci
Illustrated by Susan Hall and Bob Roper

Louis Weber, C.E.O.
Publications International, Ltd.
7373 North Cicero Avenue, Lincolnwood, Illinois 60712
Ground Floor, 59 Gloucester Place, London W1U 8JJ

Customer Service: 1-800-595-8484 or customer_service@pilbooks.com

www.pilbooks.com

Permission is never granted for commercial purposes.

Manufactured in China.

p i kids is a registered trademark of Publications International, Ltd.

8 7 6 5 4 3 2 1

ISBN-13: 978-1-4127-8926-4
ISBN-10: 1-4127-8926-5

publications international, ltd.

¡Hola! I'm Dora. Do you like soccer? Me too! This is my soccer team. We're the Golden Explorers! Today we're playing against the dinosaur team. Our team has to work together to kick the ball into the net. Will you be on our team?

My Papi is our coach! He teaches us how to play. Papi calls out directions. Sometimes he tells us to run forward and sometimes he tells us to guard the net. Papi helps us to be better soccer players. We've been practicing very hard and now we're ready to play! *¡Vamos a jugar!* Let's play soccer!

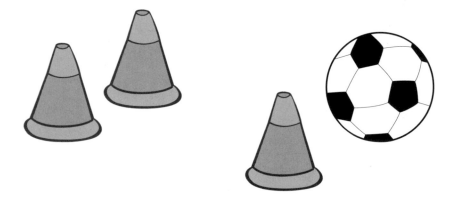

Papi throws the ball onto the field and everyone races for it. Boots is a fast runner and he gets to the ball first. Boots passes the ball to Tico. Tico kicks the ball to Diego and Diego passes the ball to me.

We have to make sure that everyone on our team gets a turn. Who hasn't kicked the ball yet? Isa! And look! She's right in front of the net. I'll pass the ball to Isa.

Isa kicks the soccer ball toward the net but the dinosaur blocks it. Wow! That dinosaur made a great save! Isa feels bad that she didn't make a goal. To make her feel better, Boots, Tico, and I cheer for Isa. We jump and clap and say, "Hooray for Isa!" because we know she tried her best.

What would you do to make Isa feel better? You're a great teammate!

Oh no! I think I hear Swiper! Do you see Swiper? There he is! He's jumping on the field and he's going to try to swipe our soccer ball. We need to stop Swiper. Say, "Swiper, no swiping." We all worked together to stop Swiper. Let's keep playing!

Hey! Our team is going to have to work together to score a goal. Who is closest to the net? Tico! I'm going to kick the ball to Tico and Tico is going to try to kick the ball into the net.

Tico did it! Our team scored a goal! Hooray! We won the soccer game! Even though they lost, the dinosaur team is happy for us!

At the end of every game, Papi asks us to say one nice thing about the other team. I think the dinosaurs are super soccer players. Boots says the dinosaur goalie is great at catching the ball. Diego thinks that they are fast runners! Isa said they are great jumpers! And Tico liked their fancy footwork. What did you like about the dinosaur team?

What a game! Everyone had a good time! I love playing soccer with you! You're a great teammate! Thanks for being on our soccer team!